幸せに長生きするための今週のメニュー

This Week's Menu for Happiness and Long Life

ロビン・ロイド

詩

中川 学

絵

ROBBIN LLOYD

poetry

GAKU NAKAGAWA

drawings

今一瞬だけ音を消して、
耳を澄まして！
季節が変わるところだから…

Be silent for a moment~
Listen!
The seasons are changing...

は じ め に

ロビン・ロイドさんはアメリカから来た音楽家です。

民族楽器の音を求めて世界中旅をして、

尺八の音に出会って日本に来て、そのままずっと住んでいます。

ライブハウスだけじゃなくて、

障害のある人やお年寄りたちの施設をまわって、

音楽の力で人をケアする活動をしている、そんな人です。

僕のお寺で時々音楽会や瞑想会をしてもらっているんですが、

ロビンさんと話すのを目的に参加する人が結構います。

参加した人はみんなちょっと元気になって帰るみたいです。

ロビンさんは時々、詩を詠みます。

まるで呼吸するみたいに、

ちょっとしたことをどんどん詩にして紙にかきとめます。

日々の暮らしや自然の、なんてことない光景を詠んだものなのに

読むと深呼吸をした時のような

背筋は伸びるんだけどいらない力が抜けるような

そんな気持ちになります。

仏教的？　なぜかそう感じます。

さてそんな詩に、どういう絵を添えたらいいんだろう。

詩を読んで不思議に思い出した情景がありました。

高校の時に見た青空の下の樹氷。

子どもたちと遊んだ鴨川の水のきらめき。

妻と見たふるような銀杏の落ち葉。

頭に浮かんだ風景の断片を、そのまま描いてみよう。

詩の内容と違うけれど、詩と絵とをぼうっと眺めていたら、

読んでくれた人だけの風景が、見えてくるかもしれない。

生きていると次々大変なことがおこって、

目の前のことも見えていない毎日ですが、

世界はやっぱりうつくしい。

そう感じられるお手伝いが、

この詩画集でできたらいいなと思っています。

中 川 学

もくじ

はじめに
-004-

月曜日
-012-

火曜日
-024-

水曜日
-036-

木曜日
-046-

金曜日
-058-

土曜日
-072-

日曜日
-086-

おわりに
-102-

幸せに長生きするための
今週のメニュー

月曜日　京都産タケノコ

火曜日　熊本産キュウリ

水曜日　佐賀産トマト

木曜日　高知産ナス

金曜日　徳島産レタス

土曜日　青森産キノコ

日曜・祝日　北海道産カボチャ

早朝、おとなりのおばあちゃんと世間話

午後、学校帰りの子どもらと笑い話

夕暮れ時、庭から聞こえるコオロギの唄

就寝～

澄みきった星空の夢

This Week's Menu
for Happiness and Long Life

Monday bamboo shoots from Kyoto
Tuesday cucumbers from Kumamoto
Wednesday tomatoes from Saga
Thursday eggplants from Kochi
Friday lettuce from Tokushima
Saturday mushrooms from Aomori
Sunday & Holiday pumpkin from Hokkaido.

Early morning greetings and a chat
With the grandma next door.

Late afternoon fun and laughter
With kids on their way back from school.

Evening serenade
With crickets in the garden,

In bed before midnight~
Clear starry-night dreams.

月 曜 日

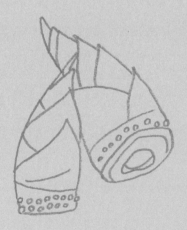

Monday

日の出前
鳥のさえずりで目覚め
谷の深さに心うたれる

Song bird wakes us
Long before the sun does~
How deep this mountain valley.

皿に残ったパンくず
朝ごはんの後
外へ出よう
小鳥の集まる場所へ
朝ごはんをふるまおう

Breadcrumbs on my plate
After a tasty breakfast.
Time to go outside
Where the birds are gathering
And make a feast for them, too.

豆腐売りのおじさん
通り過ぎ
時間と天気を知る

Tofu vendor passing by,
Telling us the time and weather.

春が来た
うきうきと歌いだすわたし
おとなりさんは耳せんをさがす

Spring's arrival
Gives me a gay song to sing.
Neighbors plug their ears!

あったらいいな
こんなワイルドな華道
丘の斜面を一面に覆う
野花のブーケ

If only a florist
Could have this touch~
Wildflower bouquets
Far and wide
Across the hillside.

春の花びらが
子どもらの上に
ふりそそぐ
哀しみなんてどこにもない

Spring blossoms
Falling like rain.
Children play~
No sadness.

見てごらん
芝の上に月明かり
上にそっと座ってごらん

Look here my friends~
There's moonlight
On the grass.
Try sitting on it!

美しい星
決して手は届かないのに
いつでもそっと心に触れる

The beauty of the stars~
While you may never
Be able to touch them,
They will always be near enough
To touch you.

笑 い の 効 用

たまには笑わなくちゃ
笑って呼吸をととのえる
呼吸をととのえて笑う

たまには泣かなくちゃ
泣くことで心が強くなる
そしてまた呼吸をととのえる

人生が喜ばしきものであればすばらしい
すべての良きことが
こぼれ落ちたなら
嘆かわしい
大切なのは
呼吸をととのえること

愛にあふれた心地よさ
あたたかさや明るさの中
恐れと冷たさ、暗闇の中
すべて同じ
呼吸が肝心
それからほほえみ

呼吸が肝心…
それからほほえみ
どこにいても
どこであっても

We All Need to
Laugh Sometimes

We all need to laugh sometimes~
To laugh and then breathe,
To breathe and laugh.

We all need to cry sometimes~
Crying strengthens the soul, too,
And then its time again
To breathe.

It's nice
When life takes a pleasant turn.
It's sad
When all the good drops out from under you.
It's important
To breathe.

In loving comfort, warmth, and light,

In grips of fear, cold, and darkness,

All the same~

The breath is first

And then the smile.

The breath is first...

And then the smile.

火曜日

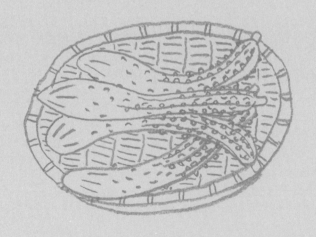

Tuesday

What Time is It?

砂漠はかつて海だった
魚はその限りない大洋を泳ぎまわった
やがて海は緑豊かな大地となり
そこで動物が草をはんだ

今はそこに砂が広がる

地球の時の流れで見れば
それほど遠くない過去に
砂漠は海だった
いつの日かこの砂漠が
再び海にかえるかもしれない

人は昨日生まれたかのよう
笑い
愛し
今日ここにあることを感謝する
明日は私たちも海になっているかもしれない

The desert was an ocean once.
Fish swam the whole expanse.
Later animals grazed there
When it turned to
Green fertile solid earth.

That is where the sand is now...

On Earth time
Not so very long ago,
The desert was an ocean,
And it could be ocean again someday.

You were born yesterday.
Laugh,
Love,
Give thanks
For where you are today...
Tomorrow
You too may be ocean.

悪天候！
風雨に打たれ人々は右往左往
足元の鳩だけは
一本の羽もみだすことなく
嵐などどこ吹く風

Terrible day!
Wind and rain
Whipping people to and fro.
Pigeons strolling under my feet~
Not a single feather ruffled.

暗雲しばし雨をもたらす
今日このごろ
朝か夕かもわからない

Dark clouds bring the rains
Early and often these days.
Whether its morning or evening now
I cannot be sure.

買い物帰り
台風のしっぽに追いたてられて
傘で家までひとっ飛び！

Walking back from the market
On the tail of a typhoon,
Umbrella flies me home!

虹の弧は
湖の東の端から
西の端の山頂まで
天の一筆

Rainbow's arc
Touching lake-side to the east,
Mountain top to the west~
Brushstrokes from heaven.

晴れの予報が
雨になり、風になり、冷え込んだ
それでも美しき一日に変わりなし

The beautiful day
That we were expecting
Turned rainy, windy, and cold~
And it was still a beautiful day.

一日の終わり
過ぎ去った時間に休息を
明日
また新しく生まれ変わる

When night falls
Put the past to rest.
Tomorrow
We will all be different people.

この世界のたくさんの人が
海を目にしたことがない
山の小川の水を味わったことがない
木にさわったことがない

人生はこれほどすてきな体験に
あふれている
さらにもっとたくさんあふれている

与えられただけのものを
返すすべが見つからず
途方にくれる
涙があふれる…

So Many People

There are so many people in our world
Who have never seen an ocean,
Never tasted from a mountain stream,
Never touched a tree.

My life has overflowed
With all of these wonderful things
And so much more.

Finding it impossible
To return as much as I've been given,
My heart fills with tears...

水 曜 日

Wednesday

ささやかな喜び

春の朝
日よけのすき間に差しこんだ太陽の光
まぶしい青空の下
みずみずしく熟したオレンジがたわわに実る木
深い谷を流れる川の向こう側
やさしい光を放つ池
波のうねりのパターンがデザインされた
古い木のテーブル
お気に入りの窓辺の席からの眺め
大切な友達の笑い顔
自分宛に配達されたグリーティングカード
メッセージの最後に「愛をこめて」

ひとつずつ色や形の違う虹
幸運にもそれに出会えること

Simple Delights to the Eye

Sunlight seeping through the window shade
On a spring morning.
Tree full of freshly ripened oranges
Under a bright, blue sky.
Soft glistening pond
On the far side of a deep river valley.
Wavy knot pattern designs
Set in an old wooden table top.
The view from your favorite window seat.
The smile of your best friend.
A greeting card in the mail
With your name on it~
Signed "love".

Each and every rainbow
That we may chance to see.

たたみを掃いて
家具のほこりをはたいて
洗濯をして
ひとっ風呂浴びる
爽快な一日！

Sweep tatami,
Dust furniture,
Wash clothes,
Scrub body~
Nice day!

庭のヘビを追い払ってと
呼び出されたが
いつしかヘビに追い回されて！

Called to chase a snake
Out of the garden,
Snake does the chasing!

きっと大目に見てくれる
おとなりさんの庭の木になる
ここらで一番おいしいみかん！

Perhaps they won't mind~
The tastiest oranges
There on my neighbor's tree!

山で道に迷う
数時間ならこのまま
誰にも見つからなければいい…

Lost in the mountains~
Hoping that no onc will find me
For a few hours...

くっきりとした夜空の星
片手いっぱいの砂漠の砂つぶを数えてみる
これまでに出会った人々の
やさしさを思い返してみる

Try to count all the stars
On a clear, crystal night~
The grains in a handful of desert sand.
Try to recall all the kindness received
From those who have passed your way
Along life's journey.

堤防で
飛び交う蛍
子らの瞳に
宿る輝き

On the riverbank~
Fireflies
Setting children's eyes aglow.

木曜日

Thursday

すべてはここに、
すべてはそこに

草むらに寝ころがる
夏の風が吹き抜ける
川岸に
やわらかな夕焼け色
皆が忙しいのは
なぜだろう？
皆が探しているものは
何なのか？
すべてはここに〜
草むらの中
夏の風が吹き抜ける
川岸
すべてはそこに〜
やわらかな
夕焼け色

It's All Here, It's All There

Laying back in the grass
With a summer breeze
On the riverbank
In a soft red-glow sunset.

What's all this running around?
What is it
That everyone is looking for?

It's all here~
In the grass
With a summer breeze
On the riverbank.

It's all there~
Soft
Red-glow
Sunset.

砂にねそべって
小さなカニを水際まで
目で追いかける

Nose down to the sand,
I follow a tiny crab
To the water's edge.

海辺の休暇
海から遠い
格安の部屋

Seaside holiday,
Cheapest room in the lodge~
Nowhere near the sea...

酷暑ゆえ
寺には参拝者も訪れず
祭壇の小さな仏さま
気持ち良さげに午睡中

Too hot!
No worshipers in the temple today.
Little Buddha on the altar
Enjoying his afternoon snooze.

風がやむと
竹はゆれ戻り
ふたたびまっすぐにのびあがる
老僧の腰は然るにあらず…

When the breeze stops
The bamboo will sway back
And straighten itself right up again~
Not so for the old monk's back...

扇風機を止めてごらん
夏のそよかぜが
扉のすぐ向こうに

Turn off the fan!
There's a summer breeze waiting
Just outside the door.

ひんやりとした午後の風が
山から吹き降りる
庭の風鈴が鳴る

Cool afternoon breeze
Sweeping down from the mountain~
Wind-bell singing in the garden.

釣り人ひとり
いびきをかきながら
川岸に体をのばす
ビールの空き缶と
釣りを続ける竿一本

Lone fisherman
Snoring,
Stretched out on the river bank.
Empty beer cans,
The pole fishing for itself.

とても小さな音

どんぐりがひとつ森の中で落ちる、
風が野に広がるススキをゆらす、
池に広がる波紋、
朝早く飛び立つ鳥の羽ばたき、
夜に降る雪、
空を満たす輝く星、
焚き火の上でコトコト煮えるスープ、
窓辺に灯るキャンドルのあかり、
ブランケットに包まれて
ぐっすり眠る赤ん坊の寝息…

Very Small Sounds

A single acorn dropping in the forest,

Breeze brushing over fields of pampas grass,

Ripples in a pond,

Bird's wings in an early morning flight,

Night falling snow,

Sky full of twinkling stars,

Pot of soup simmering on a wood fire,

Candle burning by the window sill,

Baby all bundled up in a blanket

Sound asleep...

金曜日

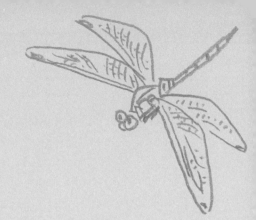

Friday

ほんの一瞬で

窓を開けて
太陽の光を入れることは
ほんの一瞬でできる
手を伸ばし
大きく広げ
新鮮な空気を胸いっぱいに吸い込み
いい朝だとつぶやいて
鳥のさえずりに耳を澄ますことは
ほんの一瞬でできる
これまで出会い、別れてきた
すべてのものに
感謝すること
「そう、生きることはすばらしい」
その思いをよびおこすこと
「愛する心」をよびさますことは
ほんの一瞬でできる

One Moment Please

It only took a moment
To open the window,
To let in the sunlight.
It only took a moment
To raise my hands,
Open my arms wide,
And take in that breath of fresh air,
To say
"Good
Morning",
And to listen to the birds
Sing their good morning songs, too.

It only takes a moment
To give thanks
For all that has come and gone.
It only takes a moment
To remember to feel
"Yes...Life is Sweet",
And to remember
To say
"I Love You".

茶友達といつものように
ポットをはさんでおしゃべり
日はすっかり短くなって
窓には霜が降りている

Here we share a pot of tea
Chatting together as we always do,
But the days seem so much shorter now~
Frost on the window.

白く、ふっくらとした
雲を追いかける
そこには秋が宿っている

Following the clouds
Suspended white and full~
Pregnant with autumn.

よく知る山道
なぜかすっかり違う顔
一枚の葉もない丸坊主

The old mountain path
Seems strangely unfamiliar...
Not a single leaf.

早起きしたけど
先を越された
やわらかく静かな冬の朝
雪に残ったキツネのあしあと

Early risers,
But not the first
On this soft, quiet winter morning.
Fox footprints in the snow.

今日はすっかり冷え込んだ
部屋の植木もふるえてる！

So very cold today~
Even the house plants are shivering!

時々人様からいただく贈り物
できれば遠慮したいもの
このみじめなる感冒よ

Sometimes I receive gifts
That I'd do better without~
This miserable cold.

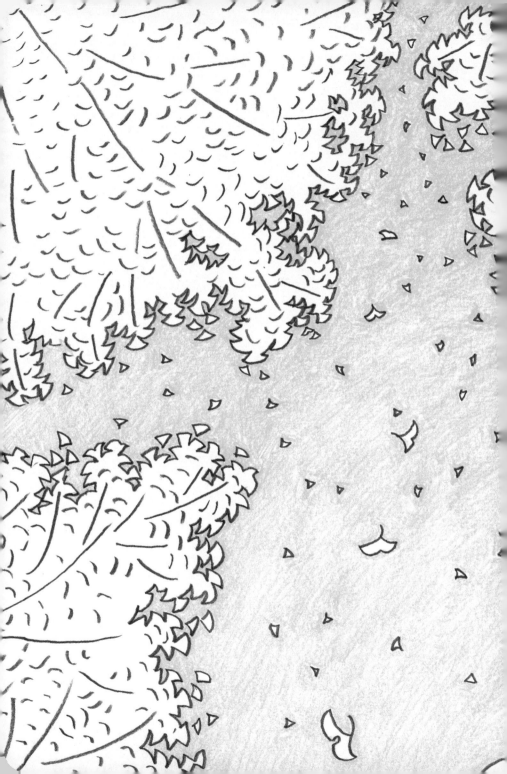

ウールのセーター

身を切る寒さ
冬の嵐が
谷間を吹きわたる
一晩で草地は氷のツンドラへ
干し草は雪にうずまり
氷のような寒風が
農場のゲートをつらぬいて
古いサイロと薪小屋の
すきま風がうなりを上げる
ひつじの群れは小屋の外

寒さにちぢこまる
一匹残らず一箇所に群れるのは
暖かな日の出の光が射し込みはじめた一角だから

この冬初めての嵐
長く厳しい寒さの夜が続く
ひつじの群れは小屋の外で
寒さにちぢこまる〜

彼らにこそウールのセーターを

Sweaters

Bitter-cold

Winter storm

Sweeping through the valley

Overnight.

Grasslands turned frozen tundra,

Haystacks covered in snow,

Icy wind breaking through the farmhouse gate,

Whistling through the cracks

Of the old silos and woodsheds.

Flock of sheep out of their stalls,

Cowering

All on the same side of the barn~

Precious rays of warm, daybreak sunshine there

Seeping in.

First winter storm,

Long bitter-cold nights to come.

Flock of sheep out of their stalls,

Cowering~

Time to give them back their sweaters.

土 曜 日

Saturday

丘 の 上 の 森

今日は休日
街を抜け出し
丘の上の森へ行く

木々は休日を知らない
鳥たちもそう

空は昨日が忙しい日であったことを知らない
雲もそう

岩々は明後日が仕事の日であることを知らない
草むらもそう

明日になっても自然は
思い悩んで眠れぬ夜を過ごしたりしない
何かを違う方法でやりなおしてみたりしない
何かを違う角度から考えなおしたりしない…

鳥、空、雲、岩々、草むらのある
丘の上の森〜
昼も夜も
夏も冬も
おだやかな日も嵐の日も
かくも生き生きとするために
知るべきことをすべて知っている
持つべきものをすべて持っている

この上なく満ち足りて生きている

Forest On the Hill

It's a holiday.
I'm out of the city
And up in the forest on the hill.

The trees don't know
It's a holiday.
The birds don't know either.

The sky doesn't know
That yesterday was a busy day.
The clouds don't know either.

The rocks don't know

That the day after tomorrow is a working day.

The grass doesn't know either.

And even when tomorrow does come,

They won't be losing sleep over anything,

Doing anything differently,

Thinking anything differently...

These birds, sky, clouds, rocks, grass,

This forest on the hill~

All through their days and nights,

Summers, winters,

Calms and storms~

They know all they need to know,

They have all they need to have

To be so very much Alive~

Blissfully Alive.

パンくずをまくおばあちゃん
雪の中でスズメとおしゃべり

Scattering bread crumbs~
Old woman chattering
With sparrows in the snow.

路上の一角にて
物乞いが寒さをしのぐため酒を飲むのも
うなずける

On the street corner
A beggar drinks to stay warm.
How can I complain?

凍えそうな夜
冬至過ぎ
耳に届くはふくろうの声…

A bitter cold night~
Winter solstice passing.
Listen for the owl...

If only for one night~

Out of our cars,

Out of our offices, factories, schools,

Out of our homes.

The whole of our world~

Lights switched off

Just long enough

To watch the moon rise...

ただ一夜

車も

オフィスも

工場も

学校も

家々も

世界中で

ほんのしばらくだけ灯りを消したなら

お月さまが昇るまで…

No need to move, no need to talk,

No need to plan, no need to change,

No need to wonder why~

Just nice to be with you,

Just like this.

動かなくても、話さなくても

なんの計画もなくても、

なにも変わらなくても、

理由なんかなくても

あなたといっしょにいるだけで

こうしているだけで

大切なこと

よく見ること

足どり軽く歩くこと

根気よく聞くこと

やさしく話すこと

笑うこと

泣くこと

深く感じること

生きることをずっと愛おしむこと

大切なこと

いつでもそれが大切

常に

It's Important

It's important
To see clearly,
To step lightly,
To listen patiently,
To speak softly,
To laugh,
To cry,
To feel deeply,
To always be in love with Life.
It's important.

日曜日

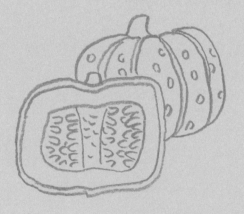

Sunday

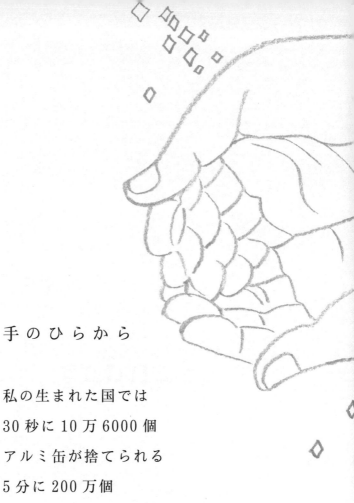

手 の ひ ら か ら

私の生まれた国では
30秒に10万6000個
アルミ缶が捨てられる
5分に200万個
ペットボトルが空になる

私は21世紀の人になりたくないな
あなたもなりたくないな
って思わない？

マグカップでコーヒーを
グラスでジュースを
おちょこで酒を
弁当には魔法瓶入りの温かいお茶を
公園の芝生の上でね
そして
冷たく透き通った
山の湧き水を
手のひらから

In the country where I was born~

Every thirty seconds

They discard 106,000 aluminum beverage cans.

Every five minutes

They finish off two million plastic beverage containers.

So you see,

I don't really want to be a modern human being.

You don't want to be a modern one either, right?

Enjoy your coffee in a mug,
Juice in a glass,
Sake in a sake cup,
Tea in a thermos with your lunch box
Out in a patch of grass in the park,
The cool, refreshing water
Of a mountain spring~
Sipping from the palm of your hand.

朝まだき
冬の枝
新雪に頭をもたげ
うれしい発見
小さなつぼみ
「春」をささやく

Early morning~
Winter branches
Heavy with new fallen snow.
Delightful surprise there, too!
Tiny buds
Whispering "spring".

寒い寒いと愚痴を言う
通りの梅の満開にさえ
気がつかぬまま行過ぎる

Complaining of the cold~
Plum blossoms across the way
Fail to catch my eye.

カーテンがゆれる
机の上の紙がはためく
風のささやきが夜気にまじる
とうとう来たか
春一番

Curtains fluttering,

Papers scattered on the desk.

Lying awake

With whispering windows in the night.

At last!

First breeze of spring.

祭りの人ごみ
露店の甘酒片手に浮かれ歩く
飲み干すごとに
財布も軽い

Cups of sweet sake

Priced for the festival crowds.

Emptying the cup

Will empty your pockets, too!

木のテーブルの上に植木がのっている
植木がいつかテーブルになるかも
もしかしたら
テーブルが芽を出し、
枝をのばし、つぼみをつけ、葉を茂らせ
もう一度植木にかえる

Green potted plant sits on wooden table.

Plant may come to be table, too.

May be

Table will sprout

Branches, buds, leaves,

And become tree again.

古い詩集を読みふける
ページに落ちる暗い影
いつしか日が暮れていた

Reading an old book of poetry~
Dark shadows across the page.
Where has the time gone?

さあ、もう一度！

専門家の最近の発表によれば
宇宙にちらばる星の数は
300,000,000,000,000,000,000,000 個
きっといくつか見落としてるよ

今夜は美しい星空
さあ、外に出て
もう一度数えよう！

Let's Count Again!

Scientists have recently reported that there are

300,000,000,000,000,000,000,000

Stars in the universe,

But I think they may have missed a few.

There's a beautiful sky out tonight.

Why don't we all go out

And count again.

Let's count again!

一　週　間

日曜日、お日さまとともに目覚める

月曜日、お月さまにみとれて夜更かし

火曜日、やかんを火にかけ、お茶をわかす

水曜日、水辺をおさんぽ

木曜日、大好きな木を抱きしめる

金曜日、金柑をほおばる

土曜日、畑で土いじりして、野菜や草花と過ごす

日曜日、またお日さまとともに目覚める

すてきな一週間をお祝いしよう

Sunday~ Wake with the sun.

Monday~ Stay up late to catch the moon.

Tuesday~ Put a kettle on the fire for tea.

Wednesday~ Take a walk along the river.

Thursday~ Hug a tree!

Friday~ Eat kumquats.

Saturday~ Plant vegetables, plant flowers.

Sunday~ Wake up with the sun again

And celebrate a splendid week gone by.

おわりに

最後まで読んでくれて、本当にありがとう。
あなたが何かを感じてはじめて、詩は、生き生きと輝きだします。
おかげで、この本がただの紙束にならずにすみました！

本を閉じる前に、一つだけ私からお願いがあります。
静かに本を読んだり、文章を書いたりするのにぴったりな
カフェや公園を知っていたら、手紙で教えてください。

私も気に入っている場所を書いて返信します。
商店街の路地裏のとあるお店とか、
芝生が目の前に広がる海辺の公園とか……。
ずっと旅して、見つけてきた私のお気に入りの場所があります。
この本の中の多くの詩も、そこから生まれました。

いつか、あなたに教えてもらった所を訪れます。
気に入ったらリストに追加するので、

今度はそのリストを見たほかの誰かが、そこを訪ねるかも！

何カ月も、何年もかかるかもしれないけれど、この本を読んだ人同士が、
こうやってつながれたら楽しいと思いませんか。

今、あなたの頭に浮かんだ場所があったら、
私宛にミシマ社まで知らせてください。

何でもオンラインでできる時代。
でも今回は、「メールではなく」切手付きの
手紙かはがきが届くのを楽しみにしています。

あなたの街でも、旅先でも、どこからでも。
I'll be waiting!

Wishing you all
Peace, Health, and Happiness,

ロ ビ ン ・ ロ イ ド

ロビン・ロイド／詩
ROBBIN LLOYD poetry

民族楽器奏者、詩人。1955年米国イリノイ州生まれ。現在は神戸を拠点に活動中。カリンバや尺八、パーカッションなど多種多様な楽器を操るマルチプレイヤーとして名高い。これまで世界50カ国以上を旅し、各地で民族楽器を学びながら出会った人々や目にした物を詩に綴っている。著書に『HAPPY BIRTHDAY Mr.B!』『1年に1度のアイスクリーム』(ともに絵・中川学)がある。

中 川 学（なかがわ・がく）／絵
GAKU NAKAGAWA drawings

1966年生まれ。京都のお寺の住職をしながら、イラストレーターの二足のわらじを履いている。“和ポップ”なイラストは国内外で定評があり、様々な書籍の挿絵や装丁を手がける。近年は絵本制作に力を入れていて、手がけた作絵に『世界でいちばん貧しい大統領のスピーチ』(汐文社)、泉鏡花『絵本 化鳥』『朱日記』(以上、国書刊行会)、『だいぶつさまのうんどうかい』『おいなりさん』(以上、アリス館)など多数。

やまがたゆうこ／翻訳
YUKO YAMAGATA translation

大阪府生まれ。高校時代にアメリカへ留学。立命館大学卒業後、京都音楽院に勤める。その後、渡英。20代でロビンの音楽に出会って以来、ロビンのエッセイ・詩の翻訳を数多く手がける。

幸 せ に 長 生 き す る た め の 今 週 の メ ニ ュ ー

2023年1月9日　初版第1刷発行

ロビン・ロイド／詩　中川学／絵

発行者　三島邦弘　発行所　ちいさいミシマ社

郵便番号　602-0861　京都市上京区新烏頭丸頭町164-3　電話　075-746-3438　FAX　075-746-3439

e-mail　hatena@mishimasha.com　URL　http://www.mishimasha.com/　振替　00160-1-372976

装丁　鈴木千佳子　印刷・製本　シナノ書籍印刷株式会社